It's Me, Until It's You

A STORY OF MEDICAL STRUGGLES, ENDLESS COURAGE AND THE LOVE THAT MADE IT ALL ENDURABLE

D.J. Connors

PAGE PUBLISHING, INC.
New York, NY

First originally published by Page Publishing, Inc. 2019

ISBN 978-1-64544-473-2 (Paperback)
ISBN 978-1-64544-475-6 (Hardcover)
ISBN 978-1-64544-474-9 (Digital)

Printed in the United States of America

This book is dedicated to
Suzanne Klose-Connors

AUTHOR'S NOTE

ALTHOUGH THIS IS A STORY about various medical conditions, it is certainly not just a medical story. This is also a story about a man and a woman, who met later in life, and shared much more than hugs and kisses and hand-holding. This is a story about trust and courage, two virtues that she possessed in abundance and, thank God, was willing to share. In the end she would not only save my life, she would save my soul.

I am not unique in what took place in my life and certainly never considered any of it special. Different maybe, but not special. My experiences pale in comparison to the many people who have suffered tragic losses or unbelievable pain. That being said, I still felt compelled to tell this story, a story, I was hesitant to tell but determined to complete.

Her story, more than mine, needed to be told, and I hope you will indulge me as I provide some background into how we ended up together. It certainly was a destination that had more to do with an ending than a beginning, but in some way I know she was waiting for me. Thank God, I showed up.

PROLOGUE

THIS STORY ACTUALLY STARTED OUT as a story about prostate cancer…my prostate cancer. I even had what I thought was a unique title, *The Walnut Closet*…the *walnut* because the prostate is often referred to as being "shaped like a walnut," and the *closet* because a lot of men are in the closet when it comes to their prostate.

I decided to "come out" because of my experiences and my realization, that I was not alone in not being informed, and I was *really* uninformed. And so, I began to write my story which, as you will see, soon became our story and then her story. Understand that from the beginning, I was not interested in interviewing doctors or hospitals, and I had and have no intention of passing judgments on either. I wasn't interested in long-winded, complicated descriptions about medical procedures or conditions. At the same time, I am cognizant of the fact that, not all prostate experiences are the same, and certainly I am not insinuating that my experiences match those of others. I simply wanted to tell a story, a true story about myself, but as happens with almost everything in life, my story turned into a different story—a love story which it should have been from the very beginning.

CONTENTS

PART ONE

It's Me

IT WAS RAINING THAT DAY, June 11, 1947, in Pittsburgh, Pennsylvania. It had to be because I was born with freckles and that is what the Irish tale says. At the time of my birth, I was bald, so my parents did not know I would have red hair. But they named me Dennis anyway. So there you have it, a perfect resemblance to *Dennis the Menace* before I had even done anything wrong. Trust me, it did not take long for me to remedy that situation. But there I was the second born of six boys in succession, followed by two beautiful sisters. I have often wondered how many children my mother would have delivered to get to that daughter that eluded her...probably eleven as that would have been a football team.

I was brought into this world by the best mother and father ever. Can you even imagine the unselfishness required just to provide for eight children? I can't. I am forever grateful for them being willing to share their lives with me—a life that I have enjoyed beyond my dreams. I grew up in a wonderful upscale community in Pittsburgh, attending a Catholic grade school and a public high school.

I majored in sports and parties, working just hard enough to stay eligible for athletics. It was, however, during my exposure to the nuns and priests that I was introduced to my guardian angels and they have made this trip with me, at times grudgingly.

After high school, I moved on to two years of college followed by four years in the U.S. Air Force, being stationed in places like Texas, Illinois, Nevada, and Thailand. It was in Nevada (Las Vegas, actually) where my high school sweetheart tracked me down. She had also attended college for two years, and now was a hostess for TWA, domiciled in Los Angeles. I had no idea what had happened to her for a couple of years until one night, she showed up. Wow. Things were about to get really interesting. It was around this time in my life when everything seemed to get a little off the rails. I was not mature enough to handle Las Vegas or the US Air Force individually, or collectively, but the powers that be felt I was. So there I was, and now I had my old girlfriend with me. Holy shit!

At some point in time, my high school sweetheart, who was now my fiancé, gathered up her belongings and made a cross-country trip to Las Vegas with her sister to setup our apartment prior to our marriage. Keep in mind…there are no cell phones back then, so I was just going on our plan when I arrived at the hotel…the hotel where she never showed up. I made the requisite phone calls, but no one had heard from her. It seems she and her sister decided to stop in Cheyenne, Wyoming, to attend "Rodeo Days" which was great, except for the fact that they didn't tell anyone, including me.

So thinking in my mind's eye, that she was in a ditch in the middle of nowhere, I decided to start drinking, something the unsuspecting tourist guest of the hotel that I charged my drinks to, probably wished it had not happened. I accelerated that bad decision with betting the limited resources I possessed, winning hundreds of dollars which eventually led to another bad decision, one that had the potential to really change my life—forever. I had enough drinks and enough money at this point to realize a change of venue was called for, so as I exited the hotel, I watched as the valet guys parked the cars and appeared to leave the keys in the vehicles (remember, this is 1969). Borrowing a car seemed plausible at this point, so I did, the operative word being *borrowed*. In any other person's mind, this would be *stealing* a car, but not in mine. I had every intention of returning the car, so the idea of stealing never occurred to me. Hell, I would never *steal* a car.

Obviously, anyone with a brain knows I was stealing, but not someone who at this point had convinced himself that his future wife was gone forever, and his life was over for all intents and purposes. I soon returned the car, not long after visiting another hotel and noticed that no one seemed to care or pay much attention to my activity. I decided at that point that it was not only easy to *borrow* a car, but actually fun, so I was soon rolling down the strip in another beautiful vehicle, forgetting completely that my fiancé had been kidnapped in another state, or not.

After completing this process several times, and drinking and gambling at various hotels, I decided to return my last car to the lot, not really realizing it was actually my "last car." Surrounded by security guards, my mind quickly admitted, *holy shit, what have I done?* I was immediately taken into custody and escorted to an office, where I would face the couple who owned the car that I had just returned to valet parking. After inspecting the car and determining that no damage had been caused, and wanting to get on with their plans, along with not wanting to be responsible for testifying at a trial to put some dumb bastard in jail, they left without pressing charges. Under any other circumstances I would have been charged with grand theft auto and sent to jail in Leavenworth, Kansas (military prison), received a dishonorable discharge and pretty much screwed up the rest of my life.

As I previously mentioned, my guardian angels (I have several) were now working overtime, and I can only say "thank you" to that couple for saving my life. As it was, I didn't get off scott free as the security people were so pissed that they notified the Air Force base and I faced immediate discipline, starting the next day as my fiancé was arriving at the hotel. Unable to be there to greet her, I had begun cleaning latrines, something that I mastered over the next thirty days. We had to scramble to get everything completed for the wedding—not to mention the number of discussions that were necessary to convince her about my sanity, but we were married at the base chapel, and spent the next year working for the airline and serving our country. We had so much fun over the next year it should have been illegal, and on one particular night, it was.

Although my wife actually commuted from Las Vegas to LA, she also worked flights back to Las Vegas often meeting celebrities and important officials. Many times, they would offer her tickets to Vegas shows, or arrange for us to have priority seating. To some degree, this was influenced by the fact that her husband was in the Air Force, and other times by dirty old men hitting on a pretty hostess. Either way, we scored a lot of tickets, one night we got to see the Righteous Brothers. Standing in line to enter the showroom, I looked down and literally saw money all over the floor. Initially confused, I soon realized others were picking up the money, and so I joined in, sticking bills in every pocket as fast as I could. Eventually we entered the show where we drank champagne, enjoyed the show, and I tipped like a crazy man.

After the show, we both headed toward our respective restrooms where I immediately entered a stall, to get a count of the money that had filled my pockets. I stopped counting at one thousand dollars, folded up the rest of the hundred dollar bills and hid them in the back of my wallet, not wanting to divulge completely our newfound wealth. Anyway, I proceeded to the blackjack table where I offered up a couple hundred dollars for chips, and within minutes two gentlemen in suits grabbed me from behind and began escorting me to an office off the casino floor. Just as we were heading in that direction, my wife sees me, and once identified, she too is escorted to a separate office area near mine.

After concealing for a period of time where I had gotten the money (my wife was telling the truth from the beginning), I finally admitted that I had found the money on the casino floor while standing in line to see the Righteous Brothers. The money we had found was counterfeit, and as I was pulling out my military ID, out pops another couple hundred bucks. Didn't seem like a big deal until the Feds told me that they suspected that the counterfeit money was being printed at my base. I came really close to fucking up big-time, until I explained that I owed money on the diamond ring I had given to my wife, and didn't want her to know that I wanted to use some of this bonanza to help pay down the balance. I know, they looked at me just like those of you who are reading this are looking at me. But before you pass judgment, think about how many times you welcomed having your taxes raised so that guys like me could get paid just enough to live on while serving my country. Yeah, I know. How about never. Well, eventually they believed our story as the counterfeit guy had literally thrown the money on the floor of the casino as he made his escape. By now, it was three or four in the morning and management felt bad that our night had been interrupted, so we were awarded a free night at the hotel, a show of our choice and dinner at our convenience. How's that for a work of art by my guardian angels?

This would not be the last time my guardian angels would visit me in Las Vegas. Actually, I guess it's a little surprising that they are in Vegas, but angels don't pick the destinations, we do. One day, me and a couple of my airmen decided to visit Lake Mead, not far from our base in North Las Vegas. Lake Mead is on the Colorado river and covers parts of both Nevada and Arizona. It was formed by the Hoover Dam and is the largest reservoir in the United States. And so, it was with that thought in mind that after a few beers, someone thought it would be a good idea to have a race. Not a race along the shore, but a race across the lake. The only intelligent part of the discussion was that we were not located on the wide part of the lake, but rather in a kind of inlet. The bad part of that discussion was that there were no boats located in the area. Before we began our swim, I decided to make a small wager that I would naturally win, convinced that I was the best swimmer in the group even without ever having seen any of the other airmen swim.

So off we went, me swimming like it was a fifty-meter sprint. Without my knowledge, everyone dropped out as I continued to accelerate forward to the middle of the lake, which is exactly where I would end up. As I stopped to survey the situation, I quickly realized it was just as far to the other side as it was to the beach, where I had begun the race. It was also at this point that I realized I had nothing left, I could not move my arms or legs, I was completely spent. You should also know that I had no life vest, which I suddenly realized as a sort of panic enveloped me. I tried to signal that I was in trouble and I think at some point my friends began looking for help, but to no avail. At this point, all I could do was tread water as I immediately thought about the ramifications of cramping. For some reason the other side of the lake appeared slightly closer, and so I got on my back and slowly, and I mean slowly, used my hands, (not arms), to move myself toward the shoreline. This took hours, but I succeeded in staying cramp free and eventually felt sand under my feet. Totally exhausted, I laid there for a long period of time, thanking my guardian angels once again for saving my life. Finally, gathering up enough strength to walk around the lake, which also took over an hour, I joined my anxious friends. Needless to say, I knew that if anything had gone wrong, I would have drowned, so once again, saved for another day. Guardian angels with me once again!

In the end, my wife and I had some good laughs regarding these experiences and settled down to more fun than we could imagine. More fun, that is, until Uncle Sam decided to fuck it all up. Welcome to Thailand. Wow, talk about culture shock. I go from a comfortable apartment in Las Vegas to Thailand where the F-4 fighter jets were flying combat missions to help support our troops in Vietnam, my brother included a Green Beret lieutenant advising the South Vietnamese Marines.

Thailand

My wife closed up our apartment and headed back to Los Angeles where she continued to fly for TWA. Her life and mine would change dramatically for the next three hundred sixty-eight days, but somehow, we managed to get through it. There were enough experiences on both sides of the world to fill another book, but for the most part she did her job and I did mine, staying out of jail and only participating in a few fights, always thinking about my return to the states.

While stationed in Thailand, I began researching Jesuit Universities, wanting to duplicate my father attending Georgetown, and my older brother graduating from Boston College. I eventually settled on Xavier University in Cincinnati, Ohio, having never actually visited either. On one hand, every place looked good from where I was sitting and on the other hand, I discovered that father O'Connor was the president of Xavier. That had to be some kind of omen, and so I applied and was accepted. Talk about a mature, rational decision that would change our lives.

Once again however, things would change for the worse. Late one night as my wife was floating around the skies toward Los Angeles, and I was sound asleep in our new Lakeshore Drive apartment in Cincinnati, I was startled awake by the sound of loud pounding at our door. As I stumbled, half awake, reaching our door with one eye open, black smoke engulfed me—shaking me to the realization that our building was on fire. The knocking came from the young ladies across the hall. They apparently had kittens on their balcony. The fire, which was just beginning in the utility and storage room below, had intensified to the point where the flames had grown to reach their balcony and were burning the kittens. The kitten's cries woke the young ladies, who then proceeded to race through the building alerting tenants and saving many lives.

Being across the hall, I was probably first to receive the alert. Our apartment was located on the first floor, although the way the building was configured you walked down a flight of stairs to exit the building, kind of a split level. Our deck, which I jumped off of was also elevated several feet off the hill, requiring me to jump to the hillside. All I managed to do was put on a pair of pants, my shoes, and jump. No car keys, no credit cards, no money, no nothing. I know what you are thinking, *what an asshole, how stupid was that?* Well you have obviously never been in a fire at 2 o'clock in the morning, sucking in smoke with every breath. You cannot believe how fast panic sets in and how limited your conscious thoughts become. In fact, my only conscious thought was—get out, fast.

After I reached the parking lot, I soon realized how bad the situation was as the building was covered in smoke and a few flames were visible through the windows. I immediately began helping other tenants climb over the decks, as by now the entire building was evacuating. Trust me, there were many people that night who helped their neighbors, more than a few that to this day, I consider heroes. I never met them, I never got their names, but I watched, and I assisted them and was amazed at their courage. Soon fire trucks arrived and began putting large amounts of water on the building. I felt a small glimmer of hope as I caught sight of our apartment, silhouetted by the light of a fireman's lamp.

Not long after that, it seemed as if everything was extinguished as the firemen began setting up fans and winding up hoses, building my hopes that at least some valuables would be spared. And just like that, hope began making a real home in my consciousness, there appeared to be an increase of black smoke, and then just as fast, the building exploded into flames. I watched from the safety of the parking lot in disbelief as the building burned against the moonlit sky and smoldered with the arrival of the morning light, creating a realization that all was lost. My wife and I, along with the other tenants, had lost everything. In a matter of hours, everything we owned was gone. I immediately thought about our wedding pictures, hell, all of our pictures. Our pictorial history now consisted of memories, all physical proof was now destroyed. Funny where your mind goes at a moment like this, but while in Thailand, I had purchased a number of tailored golf shoes—as in blue and white, brown and white, black and white—hell, they only cost ten to twenty bucks, all gone. I not only had tailor-made golf shoes, I had tailor-made suits and top coats—all gone in an instant. All of our furniture, wedding gifts, clothes, everything…Hell, I'm pissed off just writing this!

Neighbors, who I had never met, in an adjoining building were kind enough to help all of us with phone calls, coffee, and in some cases, clean clothes. My first phone call went to TWA corporate headquarters, needing to connect with my wife while feeling so sad and so emotional about passing on news that would break her heart, and break her heart it did. She arrived in Cincinnati the next day, and as we entered the apartment complex, I could hear her gasp and the look in her eyes sealed our fate. I could almost feel the wind come out of her sails. Even though I had explained everything was gone, seeing the destruction created a whole new reality. Putting this back together would require all the patience and determination we could generate, and saying it strained our relationship would be an understatement of monumental proportion.

After lots of help from family and friends, we eventually moved to a town house and settled in to welcome the birth of our wonderful son. Unfortunately, that did not sustain our marriage, and not long after we lost everything, we lost each other. Just after that, the Steelers won the Super Bowl, so all was right with the world including the fact that I had just met the love of my life, probably before the ink was dry on the divorce papers. We dated for a few years, got married and would soon be the proud parents of two beautiful daughters. After a short career in the steel industry, I moved on to a job in the mining industry with one of my customers and eventually got transferred to Pittsburgh. Back home at last. We settled in and raised our two daughters in a comfortable suburb in the South Hills of Pittsburgh, where I would sell coal mining equipment (underground mining equipment). My wife would become the best mother ever and start her own successful business.

My new position would not only involve a significant amount of travel, but also a significant amount of entertainment. Although I could spend a few hours telling those stories, one particular excursion needs to be told because once again, my guardian angels showed up. This trip with customers involved me at the last minute. It was a fishing trip to Canada that I just could not pass up. It involved a seaplane (World War II vintage) and a beautiful lake in Western Canada where we would fish for walleye and pike for three or four days. This was a fisherman's definition of heaven, and I almost went there, twice!

After a few hours of fishing on the first day, we headed with our catch to an island where our Indian guide would filet and deep-fry our fish, and we would all have a cold beer or two. As we approached the island (first boat in), I jumped onto the rocks not realizing they were covered in moss, and immediately fell into the water, the freezing water, with four layers of clothing, a ski jacket and no life preserver. Within a second, I weighed in the neighborhood of 1000 lb., so there was no pulling me out, but our guide was still at the controls of the boat and somehow managed to position it to literally push me up on the rocks and keep me from drowning. Yea, he saved my life. Other than being totally embarrassed and freezing as the other boats arrived, I had to take an hour ride back to the cabin to change into dry clothes and return to fish again, a lesson learned, and more thankful than I let on, I knew how close I had come.

After a few unforgettable days of fishing, we loaded our gear on the planes and headed back to the river in Winnipeg where we had made our departure, me in the second plane. As we entered the area where the river was located, our single engine prop plane stopped working, as in, no power. We were all now aboard a glider at a couple thousand feet watching our twenty-five-year old pilot pushing and pulling knobs. None of us realized we had actually run out of gas. I am telling you that the expression "WTF" was invented at this very moment in time. I don't give a shit what the bad language scholars from academia contend. This is exactly when it happened.

One of our customers sitting in the copilot seat looked at the pilot and said, "I noticed that the fuel gauge has been on empty ever since we took off."

At which point, the pilot responded, "Oh that gauge has not worked in years, eh." And just like that, *this* was the moment in time when "You've got to be shitting me" was first spoken—the very first time in history.

After what seemed longer than it actually was, our single engine propeller turned over and we were flying once again. The pilot apologized saying that we had hit a stronger headwind than he anticipated, which caused the plane to consume more fuel than he had planned. Another half hour passed before we landed, proceeding to the dock where we were greeted by the president of my company and the others aboard the first plane asking, "Where the hell have you guys been. We landed twenty minutes ago." The inflection in their voices insinuated that we had "lost the race" given that our departures were only minutes apart. I did not appreciate the inference that they were better than us and immediately responded, "We ran out of gas. Had it not been for that, we would have beaten you guys, eh." The appropriate analogy would present itself around that time or years after, but I remember it like it was yesterday.

Woody Paige, a sports columnist with the *Denver Post* writing an article after the Denver Broncos had defeated the Pittsburgh Steelers (my Pittsburgh Steelers) thirty-seven to thirteen quoted coach Bill Cowher as saying, "If you took away the big plays, we could have won the game."

Paige's answer was classic. "If you take away the Battles of Gettysburg, Shiloh, and Charlottesville, the burning of Atlanta, and the blockade of the southern ports, the Confederacy could have won the war. If you take away North, South, and Central America, and the Caribbean Islands, and the threats of mutiny and scurvy, Columbus could have reached India. And if you take away all the knives in the house, John and Lorena Babbitt could be a happily married couple."

My only problem with this was that I didn't write it. Not long after pulling up to the dock and defending our late arrival, vodka filled my mouth as I and the others were fully aware that this *race* could easily have had a very different outcome. All the pushing and pulling of the knobs by the pilot occurred because the primary fuel tank had run out, and the pilot was priming the secondary tank to get the engine restarted.

Fishing trip in Canada

Once again, my guardian angels stepped in to prevent what easily could have been a phone call that would have caused significant pain. It was a great trip, a great time enjoyed with really great guys, but I can't tell you how wonderful it was to walk into my house that night, hold my wife, kiss my children as they slept, and return to my American dream. No country squire, no picket fence or shaggy dog (Irish Setter), but it was close. And to ensure there are no thoughts out there that I am a complete loser, this particular part of my life (marriage) lasted over twenty years. But like all good dreams, this dream would also end.

Over the years, I had suffered my share of pain, and I certainly caused some degree myself. This pain, however, was something I had never experienced as I not only had difficulty eating, sleeping, or concentrating, I had trouble breathing. This was really bad. I officially had a broken heart, and nothing was ever going to change that, that is, of course, until two planes flew into the World Trade Center. I was on a business trip, a day after we agreed to divorce when 9/11 took place. Almost instantly, I realized what an idiot I had been, wallowing in self-pity, and I immediately began to deal with reality and the repercussions of another failed marriage. I could not think of anything other than the people and families who were suffering, and I was instantly ashamed when any thought of my situation entered my consciousness. The tragedy that had taken so many lives had saved mine, and so once again, I began starting over.

So now you know a little about me, where I came from, who was in my life, and a few of my life experiences. There would be many more to come and that part of my life would begin to unfold as I entered my fifties. Before I knew it, I was fifty-five and about to meet the love of the rest of my life. I'd like you to meet her.

PART TWO

It's Her

"HI! I AM DENNY. WHO are you?" one of the great pickup lines of all time. For some reason, I didn't care. I just wanted to meet her. I wasn't even thinking about being cool. She didn't tell me to get lost, so I asked her and her girlfriend if I could join them for a drink. It didn't take me long to get her name and number and I left them after a brief period, promising to call her for dinner. I waited the prerequisite three days and made the call.

Suzanne Klose came into my life at the exact moment that I needed her, and she needed me. Our first date was at a popular landmark restaurant where I just happened to know the recently hired hostess, and so I set it up to make a good first impression.

"Oh, are you Suzanne? Mr. Connors is waiting for you at the bar."

She never let on that she was impressed, but she was. I got a kiss in the parking lot and a promise for a second date. Suzanne was very cautious even on the second date, as she once again insisted that we meet instead of me picking her up. We actually met at a bookstore, and had coffee instead of a beer, another test to see if I could carry on a decent conversation and act normal without the aid of alcohol. We talked at length before we departed for dinner and had a wonderful evening. After our date, I proceeded to my local watering hole, where I told anyone who would listen about this wonderful lady I had met.

The third date, I was actually allowed to visit her house as I had convinced her that I was not a serial killer, and that her family would be safe. We had planned an evening of dancing and I showed up, anxious for a great night.

Suzanne actually had her mother living with her, and she was the first family member I met upon entering the house. Suzanne's father had passed away many years prior to our meeting and she had taken on the responsibility of caring for her mother. I would soon discover how much more responsibility she had taken on and how much I admired it.

The next family member I met that evening was her youngest son who shook hands and greeted me like I was indeed the serial killer his mother had feared. He made me feel certain that if I so much as kissed his mother, he would kill me. That train had already left the station, but I understood his protective behavior. After our introduction, he excused himself and disappeared to the upper floor as by then, Suzanne and I had retired to her family room for some music and drinks. She sensed I needed a drink and I immediately appreciated her understanding and her perception that I felt threatened. Not minutes after that, her son entered the family room, kissed his mother, told me it was nice to meet me (he lied), and left the house to join some friends for the evening. Alone at last, we began to relax on the sofa, and I stole a few kisses just as her son barged back into the room. I of course was sure that he was watching us and was back to kill me. Thank God, I wasn't reaching for more than a kiss. Actually, he was there to apologize for driving into my car, which was parked at the top of the driveway. Turned out no one parks at the top of the driveway. Unfortunately, Suzanne had failed to inform me of this family tradition and in his haste to meet friends, he backed up the driveway until his truck was stopped by my car. The force folded my hood like a tent. It actually looked much worse than it was, although you might get an argument from the insurance company as repair costs exceeded four thousand dollars!

An auspicious beginning for sure, but an evening that would actually change the direction of our relationship. To this day, her son is a trusted friend, but I know he has never realized the significant role he played in getting his mother and me together. How ironic, the guy that wanted to kill me actually forced me into his mother's arms. After the initial shock, I told him to proceed with his evening, not to worry, insurance would cover it and basically took the attitude that "shit happens."

Obviously, our plans for the evening had diminished to the point that we just did not feel like dancing, so we decided to hang out and listen to music. This was a turning point or at least a catalyst to our building a relationship and eventually falling in love. I honestly don't know what direction our lives would have taken had these moments never happened. But they did, and we had a great evening together and decided to continue moving forward, something I am sure her youngest son would rather have postponed instead of accelerated. And so, it was now time to get to know Suzanne Klose. Suzanne was also divorced and was coming off a long-term relationship that was very painful. She had two sons, both great guys and at the time both dating young ladies they would soon marry.

As I mentioned previously, Suzanne had her mother living with her which was really the first important indicator of her character. Take your pick: unselfish, caring, giving, loving, determined, accountable, trustworthy to a fault—you name the desirable character trait, she had them all covered and I was paying attention. Sure, she was attractive and had the most beautiful eyes in the world, not to mention a laugh that rivaled Julia Roberts, but who was counting; and she wanted me to stick around. Guardian angels at work. Suzanne did not have an easy childhood, recounting stories of washing floors in her aunt's grocery store at a young age and growing up in a neighborhood that was one of Pittsburgh's toughest. She once relayed a story about being chased by some neighborhood tough guys who had more on their minds than teasing. They backed off as she reached her front door where her brother and father took control of the situation.

Suzanne learned from a young age how to take care of herself and without question her childhood carried her through the tough times she faced as an adult. Don't get me wrong. She was very feminine and attractive, but you could tell she was no one to screw with. I often pushed her right to the limit only to quickly realize that was a direction that required a second thought. Suzanne excelled in high school and after some college, fell in love and married the good-looking neighborhood guy. They were married in the same church as their parents, the same church where they were baptized. They eventually moved to a comfortable suburban neighborhood, put down roots and raised their two sons. If I did not previously mention it, Suzanne was what I called a clean freak. I never meant that in a bad way, she was just incredible when it came to cleanliness. I am convinced that this compulsion came from her early childhood days of cleaning floors. In addition, she was taught to respect possessions, that they cost money and that the more you took care of them, the longer they would last.

Her parents, grandparents and all the adults in her formative years had instilled in her a tremendous sense of accountability. Don't get me wrong. Suzanne was not cheap, often buying the best, but she took care of things, and taught me to do the same. I mean, I too, took care of my possessions, but Suzanne upped my game. Suzanne was also extremely cautious of others' perceptions, and I don't mean in a normal way. She was fanatical about a good appearance (which I loved), good manners, and was constantly worried about what others thought, where many times my attitude was "fuck 'em."

She once relayed a story about food shopping with her two sons, the youngest around two who was eager to prove that he was the "poster child" for the terrible two's. Understanding the embarrassment of shopping with a "crazy child" and somehow getting through the checkout line, she loaded the kids in the car and drove away, leaving the groceries behind, and swearing to never eat or cook again. Prior to exiting the parking lot, and employee ran her down to inform her she had left her groceries in the cart. Reluctantly, she drove back to the entrance to gather the bags creating the very first curbside pickup, a model now employed by many top grocery chains. To this day, she has never received a royalty for her initiating this program. Suzanne was also very age conscious, which I guess fits in with her obsession over being self-conscious. After a few dates, she asked about my age, and I quickly responded with the truth... I was fifty-five. Knowing better than to ask her about her time on this earth, I waited for years before I finally was informed that she was two years older than she propagated. No big deal. I never doubted her interpretative or mathematical skills as she always looked great to me.

Her son recently shared a story of the time, he and his mother were having a few drinks at the neighborhood restaurant when an older couple, friends, or acquaintances of Suzanne's stopped by the table to exchange pleasantries. Just after Suzanne introduced her son, the woman inquired about his age. Before her son could answer, Suzanne indicated that he was twenty. As the wine for Suzanne and beer for her son arrived, the demeanor of the woman quickly changed determining that Suzanne was providing alcohol to a minor. After an uncomfortable stare, the couple proceeded on their way, leaving behind a conversation that went something like this,

"Mom, I think they know you lied about my age. You told them I am twenty when you actually know I am twenty-four."

"Honey, sometimes I lie about my age. If I told them your real age, they would think I was too young to have you."

Suzanne never gave any thought to the fact that they might think she had bought her underage son a beer, preserving her age deception inherently more important. Anyway, as her children grew, unfortunately as happens with far too many marriages, her marriage also ended in divorce and she became the primary provider and caretaker in addition to providing support for her mother. She began a real estate career working day and night to meet her responsibilities, financial as well as emotional. Suzanne did not look upon hard work as a burden. She embraced it, often referring to it as the opportunity that saved her. She saw work as an art form, it had to be perfect, not good, not excellent—perfect!

After a successful career selling real estate, she migrated toward the financial side of the business becoming a Senior Loan Officer for a large real estate firm in Pittsburgh. Not just a Senior Loan Officer, but the best in the company, and one of the best in the city. If you had financial questions, Suzanne was the "go to" for an answer. She was smart, ethical, and honest to a fault and had more awards than any person I had ever met, most stored in boxes in the attic. Humility was another character trait that I forgot to mention. Her reputation was impeccable, and all the real estate agents knew it, the customers knew it and the many notes and gifts she received from them only served to enhance their gratitude and respect.

As I think back on how wonderful this time was, realizing how lucky I was to be dating such a wonderful woman, I can't help but think about how I got in the way of her hard work and dedication. I was always asking her out, keeping her out far too late not sure how either one of us functioned. There were many dates, many different venues from sporting events to dinners to concerts to family gatherings, but somehow she managed to keep it all in perspective. After close to a year of continuous dating, I was having a beer at my local watering hole when I ran into a casual acquaintance who happened to be a six-foot-six former pitcher for the Pittsburgh Pirates. After a few beers, I began to complain about the fact that the lady I was dating was five-foot-five and me being six-foot-four bothered me. He proceeded to inform me that something like 90 percent of all females were five-foot-five or shorter, and that I was not good looking enough to limit my chances to 10 percent of the female population.

The good news is I stopped drinking, returned to rational thought the next morning and realized that the best person in my life was a five-foot-five-inch blonde, who thought the world of me and the person I could not wait to see that evening, even with a hangover. She would not only comfort me and ask that I should not drink too much but she would put on heels and dance with me all night, just to make me more comfortable—the whole time suspecting that I didn't give a shit that her feet were killing her from working all day in heels.

And so, it was around this time that I decided that I wanted to spend the rest of my life with this wonderful woman. The only question was how was I going to tell her? Or more importantly, how was I going to ask her? I decided on a simple dinner, nothing fancy, kind of like our first date. I just wanted a casual, relaxing evening and after a couple of drinks, I looked at her and said, "Suzanne, I love you. Will you marry me?" No diamond ring, no getting on my knees, no romantic presentation, just a simple statement and question all rolled into a few words.

First, there were a few tears (Suzanne never cried), then there was a profound exclamation. "I can't answer that. What the hell is wrong with you? Why are you doing this to me?" Hell, it was worse than "No", but then again it wasn't a "No." I immediately explained to her that I had considered everything, and my conclusion was her...I needed and wanted her in my life.

We had a long discussion over dinner when toward dessert, she looked at me and said "Okay, I will marry you." I was not with her the following morning, but I instinctively knew that her first conscious thought was, "What the hell did I agree to last night?" The reason I was so convinced that my instincts were correct was because she called me and told me. I was actually proud of myself for correctly anticipating the call, almost to the minute. To infer that Suzanne was cautious and calculating would insinuate that I was not prepared to defend my position. I was convinced that she was worth fighting for and I was prepared for battle. I knew she would come at me with questions and doubt, and so I drew on my past experiences, especially a time very similar to this when my previous wife questioned our future. Soon after I asked my previous wife to marry me, we packed up our belongings, rented a U-Haul and headed to Athens, West Virginia, a small college town in southern West Virginia where I had located a small apartment above a double garage, having recently been promoted to outside sales by the steel company that employed me. Our intent was to move most of our stuff to what would be our new home after our wedding, which was to take place in a few weeks. So after a four-hour drive in the rain from Cincinnati, we arrived, unloaded everything, and then carried it all up steep stairs to our beautiful apartment. We eventually settled down on the couch, opened a couple of beers, relieved that we had accomplished the feat by ourselves and looked forward to a night dreaming of our life together, which is exactly when I noticed the tears running down my future bride's face.

"I can't marry you. I just can't. I am sorry but I just cannot do this."

Without a conscious thought, I looked at her and said, "Holy shit, why didn't you say something before we carried all this shit up those steps?"

Instinctively she started laughing but more importantly she stopped crying. Years later, she confided in me that had I consoled her with something like "Oh, honey, don't worry. You are just tired. Everything will be fine." She would have ended it right then. So lesson learned and lesson remembered! I was positive Suzanne did not want to hear some lame "Oh, honey. Everything will be fine." So I looked at her and said, "Okay, I know how calculating you are, so come with me or not, but remember I have feelings, too." It was not a threat. It was a simple stating of the facts. I wanted to share the rest of my life with her and I was putting my feelings and commitment out there.

After some thought, she looked at me and said, "You are crazy, and I hate you, but yes, I will marry you."

Wow, so this incredible woman was going to marry me, the guy with enough baggage to shut down every conveyor belt at every airport in the country and fifty-five years old to boot or fifty-three in Suzanne years. I have often reflected on that day, the how's and why's and everything that had to happen to get to that moment in time. Every question asked going unanswered and every thought confusing me more after it than before. The only thing that was clear was how thankful I was and how once again my guardian angels showed up to save me. Little did I know that our future would not only involve angels, it would involve miracles.

PART THREE

It's Us

SUZANNE AND I WERE MARRIED on June 11, 2004, with the ceremony taking place at a country inn near Pittsburgh where we utilized the outdoor pavilion for our vows and a small reception. It was a beautiful setting and I'm sure if we all could have seen it, we all would have agreed. The problem was we couldn't see it, as the worst and hardest rainstorm to ever hit Western Pennsylvania ruined our view. Some called it good luck, while others said it was really bad luck. I, for one, would never forget it…not because of the monsoon, but rather because it was my birthday, my 57th to be exact. Suzanne was not exactly elated about getting hitched on my birthday but acquiesced realizing I was protecting against ever forgetting an anniversary again, something that unfortunately I had been stupid enough to have had to defend in the past. We had a great service and a reception for a small group of family and friends including our five children. Suzanne's two sons walked her down the path to the pavilion and it was at that moment that I knew this was a good decision.

I learned later that Suzanne also had a *moment* just before she left the inn to walk down the path telling her maid-of honor that she was having second thoughts. Thank God, I was not standing next to her as we may have decided to just have a party and forget the marriage part. It wasn't that we did not love each other, it was just a big step for both of us. First of all, we were both older, we had only known each other for a little over a year, her mother and my two daughters were going to live with us, and we had never lived together. So yea, we were both apprehensive, but we had made a commitment, so It was time to follow through. After all, we had invested considerable time into preparing for our next home.

The process of determining where we were going to live was difficult, actually it was hell. Suzanne owned a house, and I owned a house and neither of us wanted to move to the other's house. Looking back, I should have capitulated and moved into Suzanne's house, but she owned a ranch and I disliked ranch houses. I really made things more difficult for her and her mother, and I honestly would take that decision back if I could, but I can't, and so we both put our respective houses up for sale and began looking for our new home. I think I mentioned earlier how Suzanne was meticulous and the closest thing to a perfectionist that I had ever seen. When it came to shopping for, and evaluating new homes she was worse. For some strange reason, I had forgotten that she was a real estate agent before she got into the financial end of the business and that proved to be almost more than I could take. In my business world at the time we would call it paralysis by analysis and my definition of due diligence could not hold a candle to hers.

As a matter of fact, my candle was about to go out just as we stumbled upon our new home. We were actually on our way to look at another house, when a lady came out of her house and put a For Sale by Owner sign in her front yard. The house was very nice from the front, but I wanted to get a look inside and insisted that we stop. Suzanne agreed, reluctantly, as it wasn't exactly what she was looking for. Once inside, I knew "it was exactly what I was looking for," complete with a bay window and back deck overlooking the 18th tee and 10th green of the golf course, which just happened to be part of the neighborhood we were evaluating. After giving sufficient thought (about five seconds) to the idea of having a putting green almost in my backyard, I insisted on giving the woman sufficient hand money to at least hold the house while my wife and I discussed pluses and minuses. I pulled the sign out of the yard as we departed. To say that Suzanne was upset would be kind, she was furious as I had given up any negotiating leverage we had (I felt the house was going to be gone) and could not figure out how I could be that stupid. I basically was saying that I was right and the lady who had spent over twenty years in the real estate business was wrong. I had not even given her a chance to "do her thing." Of course, that only mattered if we bought the house. If we walked away, no harm, no foul.

So time for a drink and a long discussion. "I seriously can't believe you just did that, didn't you think it was important to talk about before you offered hand money, holy shit. I can't believe you did that."

"Suzanne this is a great neighborhood, all the amenities match what we are looking for, it's in our price range, it's a great house and it just so happens to be sitting on a golf course. What is not to like?"

Our marriage plans almost ended that day, but somehow we got through it, negotiated a slightly lower price and bought the house. Suzanne never really accepted it but over time it became our home and one beautiful summer evening, years later (yea, it took that long) she looked at me sitting on our deck and said, "You know, I really love this place." At that exact moment in time it no longer mattered if I ever got to heaven. And so, Suzanne sold her house and I sold mine, and we all moved into our new home in June of 2004 shortly after our wedding—on my birthday—or did I already mention that? Not long after moving in, my oldest daughter and I were having a discussion when she offered up a profound explanation concerning my marriage. "You know Dad, being married three times doesn't really sound that bad until you say it out loud!" If you can't find the humor in that, read another book. She was right, and I needed to accept the fact that this was "my third marriage." I often looked back and pondered the teachings of the nuns and priests and the sacrament of matrimony, and at this point in my life felt I had failed them. At the same time, I was in love with this woman and I needed to make a commitment.

One of my favorite songs or lines in a song are the words or lyrics from a Dionne Warwick recording which includes the verse "A fool will lose tomorrow looking back at yesterday." I probably exemplify those words, and although I am not insinuating I don't respect the past, it is only the present and future that interest me. I have wonderful memories and cherish every moment of my life, but I don't live there. And so, Suzanne and I settled down to a life together in our new home. Proud of what we had overcome and accomplished, soon realizing that everything had worked out for the good.

Suzanne continued her work in the mortgage business, and I continued my career in Industrial Sales. We had many years of family gatherings at the house, great vacations, and shared many memorable days and nights. Everything wasn't perfect, sometimes difficult molding two families together, but for the most part we had a great time. Over the next few years, we had a number of weddings as our three sons, met and married three wonderful women, all now a part of our family. Along the way, we lost Suzanne's mother who had done an incredible job of trying her best to provide us with privacy, not wanting to be a burden, and always putting our comfort ahead of hers. Probably my biggest regret during the years that she lived with us was not including her more in my life. We shared family times and we always made sure she was involved, but if I had to do it over again I would have spent more personal time with her.

Suzanne and I at her son's wedding

Eventually grandchildren began arriving and on May 2, 2007, Suzanne's first grandchild (a boy) arrived joining our family just when she needed it most. I may be wrong, but I think other than the birth of her two sons it was the happiest day of her life and she would go on to prove it by being the most incredible grandmother ever.

Suzanne with first grandchild

Before we could celebrate the marriage of my two daughters, we would begin to face what would become the most difficult times of our lives. It was late 2009 when after a routine physical I was notified that my PSA had elevated to a level of concern.

Without getting too technical, let me give you a brief definition for PSA. PSA stands for Prostate Specific

43

Antigen, which is a protein produced by the prostate gland. While most PSA is carried out of the body in semen, some escapes into the blood stream, and that then can be used to test for problems in the prostate, like an enlarged prostate or prostate cancer.

My PSA was 17.41 well above my first reading of 3.4, so I opted for a second test. The result was 19.75, not the second opinion I was looking for. In the end, it didn't make any difference which test results they used. The outcome was the same. "You need to get a biopsy of your prostate." Fuck! Well, allow me in hindsight and in a humble opinion to explain how important the prostate is. The prostate gland is so important that you should be aware of it at thirty. Actually, it probably would be a good idea if you knew what it was in your twenties. Honestly, it would not hurt to be aware of it in your teens! The real truth is that when you are born, your doctor should shove his/her finger up your ass and describe to you what he or she is feeling, then tell you to never, ever, *ever, ever, ever* forget it. Of course, I am not sure it is fully developed at birth, but you get the picture. The meeting to review the results of my biopsy took place in October of 2009 with my doctor and my wife. He told us I had a little cancer which was like telling a woman she was a little pregnant. Turned out, I had more than "a little" cancer. The measurement used to determine the extent of cancer in the prostate is called a Gleason score. The score is made by a pathologist who examines the biopsied tissue. The score is made up of two grades, the most common grade and the worst grade. My scores were a six and a nine which means I scored three and three in one quadrant (not too bad) and a four and five in the other (not too good). So given my high PSA level and a Gleason score of nine (on a scale of ten), my situation was not good.

The stress from that meeting is etched in my memory like almost nothing else I have ever experienced, and the look on my wife's face haunts me to this day. She was shaken. We both were. We left the office without saying a word until my wife asked, "Where are we going and what are we going to do?"

The first part was easy to answer. "We are going to get a drink or twenty." The second part was a little more difficult. "I have no clue." As we discussed the options the doctor had presented, none of which were good, we eventually eliminated everything except surgery. We decided the most important course of action was to get the cancer out. What we soon discovered, however, was that it was a little more complicated. First you had to prove that the cancer was totally confined within the prostate and for the hundredth time, I uttered the infamous words, "Holy shit. I didn't know that." In order to qualify for a radical prostatectomy, the doctors must be at least 99 percent sure that the cancer is contained. The tests for this are not all that difficult (CT scans, bone scans, etc.) but the waiting for the results was overwhelming. I may not have mentioned this but having a sense of humor is paramount to almost everything I experienced. So after my bone scan, I asked the technician if I could see my skeleton and it instantly gave me a deep appreciation for skin and organs!

Having decided on a radical prostatectomy not only involved a number of tests, we also had to decide if robotic or manual surgery was the course we wanted to take. We chose to trust the hands and fingers of an experienced surgeon rather than a robot (directed by an experienced surgeon) because of the importance of saving nerves and the complications that presents to having a future sex life. But first we had to pass all the tests. After months of tests and waiting, we were notified that I had met all the requirements. They were 99 percent sure the cancer was contained. My prostate surgery was scheduled for December 18, 2009. Merry Christmas! The surgery went well, except for the fact that I forgot to tell my surgeon…I have a bad back. Not that it would have made a difference as far as the surgery was concerned, but I found out after surgery, you are positioned so that your lower abdomen is comfortably accessible for the surgeon. In other words, they fold you in half, backwards, for a couple of hours. WTF! My recovery was slowed by two things: back pain and no drugs…sorry three things…I had a tube (catheter) shoved up my dick! My wife stayed overnight in my room for two reasons. First, she was concerned I would kill someone to get my hands on some drugs, and second, that I would kill myself. She made the right decision on both counts.

After getting through the night (no sleep), the surgeon visited the next morning to tell us that everything had gone well except for one little problem. During the surgery, they also took out several lymph nodes. I guess this is similar to a woman's breast surgery so that they can examine the surrounding tissue to ensure the cancer was contained. In my case, they examined twenty-five lymph nodes and one showed positive for cancer, meaning the CANCER WAS OUT! Keep in mind that I didn't feel really well the morning after surgery, so getting this news was a little bit of a strain on my system. My wife saw it coming and left the room before I blew up. WTF was the best I could muster. Not my best moment! My mind was spinning at this point around the fact that we did not "get the cancer out." I was still pissed off that I had a tube up my dick, and now they tell me (us) that I still have prostate cancer and that the catheter had to stay in for eleven days. Eleven days…oh my god… Christmas was six days away.

This was one of several points where I know my wife saved my life, at least for eleven days. I had heard about catheters, but never thought I would actually be a person who used one…one of those little details that my doctor failed to mention and for good reason. He knew that I would kill him. He also knew that it would be inserted during or after surgery when I was unconscious, so I really had no say in the matter. I am a pain in the ass when I get a common cold, so I am sure you can picture my sparkling personality with a tube up my dick during Christmas. I was positive that my wife would leave me as soon as I could breathe normally. She did not leave me, but I am positive she gave it some serious consideration. During those eleven days, we talked at length about "where do we go from here." It was difficult to figure that out given our lack of information, but we knew once the catheter was removed and I gained some sanity, we could begin to make some intelligent decisions. It just happened that day was New Year's Eve, and if ever we were ready to party, this was it. We arrived at the hospital early afternoon and I entered the doctor's office while my wife waited anxiously in the adjoining room. I was directed to a small examining type room where I was introduced to a doctor, I had never met…I guess the junior guy who gets stuck removing catheters.

To this day, I am not sure if there is anything that compares to having a catheter removed after eleven days. I have thought about the best sex I have ever had, and I might actually vote the catheter removal as the best feeling ever. I don't mean to insinuate physically better, but I know I mentally experienced some kind of an orgasmic event. Not an event I ever want to experience again any time soon, but an event nonetheless. We exited the hospital feeling great and I asked my wife to stop at a local watering hole so that we could get a jump on our New Year's celebration. After one beer, we headed for home where I passed out and slept for eighteen hours. Happy New Year! There was good reason to be exhausted. I had not had a decent night's sleep in over two weeks, and my wife did not get much more. If she wasn't sleeping, she was thanking God for getting her to this point without killing her husband. She nursed me through the whole process, and I am eternally grateful. Slowly, the days passed and I gained more strength although full recovery took months. I eventually worked my way back to a fairly normal life. Back to work, helping around the house, spending time with the grandkids who invariably would find their way to putting either their knee or their foot into my groin. To this day, I marvel at the joy a two-year-old gets from seeing a grown man cry.

It was now time to meet with the doctors to formulate a game plan to attack the cancer cells that were basically floating around in my body. After surgery, I really did not fully understand the implications of the one lymph node testing positive for cancer although I certainly knew it was not good. It was now time to "get the rest of the story." There were two really important subjects that we covered in that meeting. The first thing we learned was that one of the nerves, (the nerves we were so concerned about), attached to the prostate, (or running through it), was determined to be cancerous and had to be removed. The other nerve, however, was okay. Specifically, "the left unilateral nerve was spared but the right was non-nerve sparing." While writing this, I decided a more technical explanation was required and so I googled it, and here is what I found courtesy of Healthline Medical, "Two sets of nerves supply the corpora cavernosa, which are known as the greater and lesser cavernous nerves. The nerves of the prostatic plexies are distributed to the corpora cavernosa of the urethra and the penis, which are areas of expandable tissue that fill with blood during sexual arousal, creating a penile erection." I hope now you completely understand why I did not want to interview doctors and hospitals. We don't really think about the male reproductive system that much. Women have a monopoly on that, but believe me, there is some really complex shit going on that I sure didn't know. Maybe I am alone with this perception, but I doubt it. Anyway, the fact that one of my nerves was spared meant that I, (we), would at least have a fighting chance at a future sex life. I might require some help from a little blue pill or another stimulant, but at least I had a chance. The second topic we discussed, and one that was just as important, was that one little lymph node that tested positive. After all the stress, after all the tests, after surgery, after everything we had been through, I still had prostate cancer. I quickly came to realize over the months and years that followed that the fight was not over. It really had just begun.

My wife realized almost immediately, that this was a major problem where I was naïve and didn't think it would be that difficult to "finish this off." I don't think I fully grasped the significance of what I was being told. Certainly, I had been through the worst, so how difficult could it be to take care of this one little lymph node? I got that answer almost immediately—really difficult! The first step that needed to be taken care of was to get another blood test to check what level of PSA was still in my body. The test revealed a PSA of around .005, which my new post-operative doctor described as negligible, not zero, which it most likely would have been had it not gotten out, but not bad. At that point, we took a wait and see approach and I continued to be tested every month. I should note here that you are not hearing about any chemotherapy or radiation treatment because I had cancer cells basically floating around in my body and nothing had metastasized to my bones or other organs. There are cases where these treatments are used but not in my particular case…that is, not until I requested it, which I will explain later.

As the months passed and my tests continued, my PSA eventually began to increase. This was caused by the growth of male hormones called androgens, the most common androgen being testosterone. In other words, the cancer cells were growing (feeding) off of the androgen (testosterone). I don't remember the exact incremental increases, but they went something like this: .005 to .010 to .125 to 1.0 to finally reaching a point where we needed to stop the progression. So, just when I started feeling like a man again, I was informed that I needed to begin treatment to stop or limit the growth of the cancer. My doctor told me I needed to begin hormone replacement therapy. I would receive a shot every three months and hopefully we would see signs that the cancer was retreating. Hormone replacement therapy is one name given to this treatment. It is also called hormone therapy, or androgen deprivation therapy. I also had a name for it which wasn't quite as docile as hormone replacement therapy! I called it "YJFUTROML" or "You Just Fucked Up the Rest of My Life!" It sounds more like a town in Afghanistan, but trust me, I was closer to the truth than the doctors or drug company that came up with Hormone replacement therapy. I was born and raised a Catholic and I have always believed that God was going to punish me for all the bad shit I had done in my life. There actually is enough there for some pretty serious discipline, so I have always prepared for something. But I have questioned, almost from the beginning, that we might be taking this to an extreme!

Metaphorically speaking, I was not only being turned into a woman, I was being turned into a woman in menopause. Trust me, I have experienced that up close, so I had every reason to consider the punishment excessive! Anyway, after a couple of shots, my side effects started showing up. You know how your anxiety levels rise when you see a drug commercial on TV, and they casually list the side effects at the conclusion and you sit there and think, "Shit, I would rather be dead than go through all of that." Well, for the most part, you really won't experience all those side effects. Regulations insist that they declare them…not exactly a good marketing campaign. My drugs also listed side effects although I never actually saw them in writing, at least as they related to the shots I was receiving. My doctor did, however, review them with me and they included: erectile dysfunction, loss of interest in sex (lowered libido), hot flashes, loss of muscle mass and physical strength, bloating, mood swings, and growth of breast tissue. Would you like me to repeat those so that you can get a complete appreciation for exactly what my immediate future was shaping up to look like? I didn't think so. I'm not exactly sure what kind of sliding scale or score God puts on questionable behavior, but I know I never killed anyone, so I think all of this was a little over the top. And unlike those TV commercials where the listed side effects don't always present themselves, mine for the most part all showed up, with the possible exception of mood swings although some would even argue that. Hell, how could I not have mood swings?

It was not an easy time, and it certainly was not something to laugh about although the hot flashes, for some reason, made the exceptions list. My wife was very considerate, and she certainly knew how serious these side effects were. She was sensitive to my frustrations…the hot flashes, however, were different. She knew they were difficult and bothered me, but she just could not hold back when I would let out a "I can't fucking stand this shit anymore," with sweat running down my face. She would laugh sometimes bordering on hysteria. I will tell you flat out that one of the things that I loved the most about my wife was her laugh. It was infectious, so much so that her laughing at me soon caused me to start laughing at myself. To this day, with hot flashes more intense than ever, I find myself laughing, when I should be crying. This particular dimension of what transpired in our marriage and relationship is all part of her not only saving my life but saving my soul. These were difficult times and without her I am unable to tell this story, a story back then that we thought only involved me. It would not be long before we learned how much more we would have to endure and how much of that would involve her.

A few months after recovering from prostate surgery I returned to work, and all was good until it snowed like hell, one day in February and I had to snow blow the driveway so that my wife and I could get out for work. After completing the task, I returned to the family room where Suzanne was having her first cup of required coffee. "Hey, I think I have a problem." I said, "My chest really hurts." I suspected acid reflux as I had suffered from it for years, but eventually it dissipated and she left for her office, and I showered and proceeded to my office for a meeting. At this point in my career I was Director of Sales and one of our salesmen entered my office just as the chest pains returned. I tried to convince him it was acid reflux, but he insisted I get my ass to the hospital, probably saving my life.

Discretion being the better part of valor, I left the office and drove to the hospital thinking the whole way I was not going to see tomorrow or even the rest of the day. I left a message for my wife on her cell phone and soon I was admitted, the whole time insisting it was just acid reflux but knowing something was different. Suzanne soon arrived after I was checked in and we proceeded to a private room. The blood tests indicated that I indeed had a problem with my heart although not serious enough that it couldn't wait until the next morning when a heart catheterization was scheduled. The nurses continued to monitor my blood throughout the night deciding eventually that I needed to be moved to the front of the line for surgery. I had insisted the night before that my wife go home and get some rest, as we didn't originally plan for a 7:00 a.m. catheterization, causing her to miss my being taken in for surgery.

Having never experienced this procedure, I was shocked to learn that I would be awake. I could literally watch the catheterization on a computer screen, and they even gave me something relaxing so that I was calm...I was actually anticipating popcorn! They entered through my groin traveling up to my heart basically searching for blockages, which they found immediately. At this point of what they call an angioplasty, which is a balloon tipped catheter used to open the artery, the artery opens, blood begins to flow, and a stent is then inserted to ensure the artery stays open. The balloon is then deflated and removed. Wow, this was really amazing and as I entered the recovery area medical technology consumed my every thought. My wife soon joined me and we both agreed that once again, my guardian angels were with me. I was soon notified by the doctor that my artery was 95 percent blocked and that I indeed had suffered a mild heart attack, mild meaning that I had lost approximately 10 percent of my heart muscle.

After a few days I recovered to work and settled down to a normal schedule, happy that I felt better and thrilled that I had dodged another bullet. We soon moved from February to April when I received what I initially thought was a prank call. My wife had gone in for a routine checkup and the doctor did not like what he was hearing from the other end of the stethoscope. She was immediately sent to the local hospital where the cardiologist discovered that Suzanne's heart valve was leaking, and that she had an aortic aneurysm. This call was no prank. Suzanne was crying on the other end of the phone and she needed me, immediately. I could not believe my ears as I heard her say "They just ran some tests and I have a heart aneurysm and my heart valve is leaking." Suzanne was in terrific shape, she walked miles daily, drank moderately, and was under weight for her height. There had never been a problem with her heart. But she was in trouble and as we listened to the doctor it was clear that her condition was serious. We needed to move quickly as this was not something you let linger. We needed answers to a bucket full of questions and fast.

It was determined that Suzanne was born with what they call a bicuspid aortic valve which is a valve that only contains two leaflets (or flaps) instead of the normal three. These valves are subject to leakage making them susceptible to aneurysm formation. As I mentioned previously, Suzanne was a detail person and after we overcame the initial shock, we began gathering information including researching hospitals and surgeons around the country, quickly determining the Cleveland clinic was far and away, the most advanced on valve replacement. Soon, however, a surgeon in Pittsburgh became the front runner not only for his experience (hundreds of surgeries) but also from our meetings. Suzanne trusted him as did I, and we soon formed a relationship that would ultimately lead to Suzanne having the surgery in Pittsburgh. And so, we all gathered at the hospital in early April knowing that this surgery would be lifesaving. Suzanne and I rose very early without much or any sleep and joined all our children for the toughest day of our lives, Suzanne needing all of us by her side. I can't remember how long the surgery took, but it was many hours before we (I) were able to see her, the surgeon explaining that everything went well and that he was pleased with the results.

The nurses taking care of Suzanne in the intensive care unit explained to all of us that Suzanne was doing fine but was obviously hooked up to a considerable amount of equipment, would not be able to talk, and that we needed to be prepared for seeing a loved one in this condition. I was first to visit her, being her husband, and I have no way of describing what I felt as I entered the cubicle. My first conscious thought after I grabbed her hand and kissed her forehead was my wife will never ever survive this, and the look in her eyes was simply "help me" which I was helpless to do. Helpless doesn't come close but I was convinced that no one could survive what I was witnessing. I was shocked at how calm all the nurses were, later that night showing me my wife's new valve working perfectly—a pig valve— holy shit! Eventually all our children visited Suzanne and although we did not discuss our feelings I'm sure they shared my concerns. This was unbelievable stuff, and between all the monitors and tubes running into and out of her body there was just no way our Suzanne would ever be the same. That is until the following morning.

After grabbing a few hours of sleep and a change of clothes I returned to the hospital early the next morning finding Suzanne in a private room sitting up in bed and anxious to walk. No longer tethered to all the equipment and monitors and now able to talk, she made it abundantly clear to me and the nurses that she needed to get up and walk. "Get up and walk? What the fuck is wrong with you woman! You could have died less than twenty-four hours ago, and you need to rest." If there was ever a moment in my life where I felt like a complete pussy it was then, as she was ready to move forward after her surgery and a mere four months earlier I complained incessantly after mine, that it was "too soon to walk and please leave me the fuck alone."

Her determination amazed me, and I think even the nurses who deal with these recoveries on a daily basis. If it wasn't that day, it was the next when I helped her navigate the corridors of the unit trying to reach a goal that would eventually get her discharged. She had to prove to the doctors and nurses that she could walk a required distance and climb a set number of steps to ultimately get approval to "go home." I can't remember exactly but I think she set some kind of record for leaving the hospital after valve replacement surgery. Talk about determination. I was shocked, at the same time realizing who I was dealing with. Suzanne wanted to go home even though her overly cautious husband was insistent on a longer stay. "I am fine, let's go. Doctor tell him, I am okay to leave." It had only been a couple of days since I thought my wife would not survive let alone leave the hospital. We were all shocked that she had overcome such an unimaginable health problem telling me, "I told you I could do this" as I helped her into the car. This was a medical miracle and I'm not sure I have ever been prouder of anyone. You want to talk about tough—this is tough!

It took a few weeks to get totally back to normal but before long, we were making plans, and in her case, keeping promises. Suzanne had promised both of my daughters that she would dance at their weddings, one a little over a month away, the other a few months after that. Sure enough, she danced at both weddings, doing so without the knowledge of many of the guests and thrilled that she had kept her promise. Obviously the second wedding "promise kept" was not as significant as the first given the extended time involved, but she and I loved every moment she was in my arms, both laughing, and thinking identical thoughts without saying a word. After getting through another two weddings things began to settle down. Hell, they had to. In less than a year, we had experienced prostate cancer, a heart attack, heart valve replacement surgery; and two weddings all before the end of the 2010 summer.

Other than a couple of heart catheterizations for me over the next couple of years, we really began enjoying our time together with more grandchildren arriving and lots of family get-togethers. I believe I mentioned that Suzanne was a dedicated walker, walking miles every day. She typically walked the neighborhood, many times, walking the golf course, and as much as I liked golf, I had no chance of keeping up with her the few times I tried. She eventually hooked up with a few neighbors, walking most mornings, some afternoons or evenings several times a week. A few years after her surgery she was out walking with her regular group when she experienced a dizzy spell and fell, cutting her head on a curb. Her walking mates called an ambulance, which she was being loaded into just as I arrived, having initially gone to the wrong cul-de-sac. Now conscious, she was pissed that she had to go to the hospital, but I thanked her friends and followed the ambulance, soon dealing with a doctor who was not ready for Suzanne. "I am fine, I don't need to stay overnight, please just let me go home." She had to sign a release, or rather I did to get her released. They had run tests, found nothing so "We are leaving."

This was not the first time an "episode" like this had taken place. Twice before while working out on our tread-mill she had gotten dizzy, fell to the floor and called for me to help. Every time we would just sit there on the floor, the pain or symptoms would dissipate, and she would look at me and say, "I am fine." On one occasion, I actually told her no, she was not fine and that we were going to the hospital. To prove me wrong she got back on the treadmill and had no problem walking faster than I could run. I just walked away not understanding anything as she looked at me and smiled. The other side of that coin was that she had told friends at work that she was concerned about driving her grandchildren, not totally convinced that a dizzy spell might not occur while driving. She never shared this concern with me. If I so much as suggested going back to the hospital, she pushed me away. She was never going back, so like an idiot, I complied.

April 8, 2013 arrived like any other day, only this morning was more beautiful and warmer than most for this time of year in Pittsburgh. We talked in the kitchen prior to leaving for work, Suzanne with the mandatory coffee and me with my cereal and banana, when she asked if I would walk with her after work. It was not only a little unusual how warm it was, it was unusual for her to ask me to walk with her after work. I preferred the elliptical machine in our house as it put less pressure on my knees. In addition to not really wanting to walk, I had good reason not to as the NCAA basketball championship game was that night. The truth is that what I really wanted to do was take her out to a bar, have dinner, and watch the game. For some reason, probably guilt, I said, "sure" and was pissed the rest of the day. How selfish was that…Suzanne arrived home a little after six o'clock not long after I entered the house. "Are you going to walk with me?" was the first thing out of her mouth.

"Absolutely." As I gathered my shoes and she headed upstairs to change. We headed out the door to what was a beautiful spring evening, Suzanne leading the way as she liked being in control.

As we entered the street, Suzanne turned left instead of to the right, which would have provided a more level surface. Within a couple hundred yards, Suzanne got dizzy and I helped her to a neighbor's lawn. This was exactly what had happened in the past, but she had walked many times after those "episodes" with no significant problems, but here we were again experiencing the exact same thing. We sat there as we had before, me insisting on calling 911, and her telling me to wait that her discomfort would pass. After saying no to everything, she eventually accepted a bottle of water from a concerned neighbor after turning down help from several cars that had stopped to offer assistance. Eventually Suzanne said *yes* to another passing vehicle as she "wanted to go home," so we helped her into the front seat of the SUV, me behind her in the back seat. At that point, I began dialing 911 and as we pulled up in front of our house she literally fell out into my arms.

I knew immediately this "episode" was different, although I was not present the time she hit her head, but every other time she talked with me and now she was not talking or listening. I remember calling 911 a second time as it seemed to take forever when I'm sure it was only minutes. As instructed, I laid her on her right side and laid down beside her deciding to breathe into her mouth as she was not listening to my "breathe Suzanne, breathe" commands. The paramedics finally arrived, administered an intravenous and shocked her heart almost simultaneously, then loaded her into the ambulance and headed for the hospital, fast. I grabbed the keys to my car, my neighbor offering to watch the house and followed the ambulance at high speeds. Somehow, I managed to call her youngest son telling him to get his brother and get to the hospital, saying that Suzanne was in trouble. Although I knew it was really bad, I could not bring myself to say much more than just get there—fast.

Her oldest son arrived not long after they had escorted me to a private waiting room. Not long after that, a hospital spokesperson entered the room and informed us that Suzanne had passed away. "I'm sorry, what did you say?" Was the only thing I could say, knowing exactly what she had said. I'm not sure if her son was holding me up or I was holding him up, but disbelief had totally consumed us and we both broke. About that time, her youngest son entered the room, and without saying a word but seeing us holding each other, knew immediately. As he repeated "no" it was all I could do to comfort him—how the hell do you do that...

As I wrote this part of the story, having feared it from the day I started this project, I can tell you the images are as clear as if these moments happened yesterday, when in fact we are approaching five years. The pain was unbearable and conscious or clear thoughts were almost impossible, and yet at some point the hospital offered to bring Suzanne into an adjoining room so that we could visit with her. Although those hours were filled with more tears and pain than I can adequately describe, that time with her was vital, for all of us. We kissed her, hugged her, held her hand, and cried harder than we had ever cried in our lives. We had lost our wife, our mother, our grandmother, our mother-in-law, our stepmother, and our friend, in my case, my best friend. In a matter of a few hours from our conversation in our kitchen, Suzanne was gone—forever.

Eventually we left the hospital and gathered at our house in the early morning hours, all feeling guilty that we had to leave Suzanne. I initially had asked for a complete autopsy but hated the thought of her being dissected so I called her surgeon and asked him if he would examine her heart so that we could get some idea as to what happened. I knew I needed to know and assumed everyone else did also. After a few days, he called to inform me that scar tissue had built up where the valve was attached (stitched) to the aortic shelf and a sort of flap (scar tissue) had closed her valve. He had seen this exact thing once before in all the surgeries he had performed, but that patient exhibited enough symptoms that it was corrected with another surgery.

Somehow all those "episodes" that Suzanne had experienced corrected themselves, somehow the scar tissue moved or shifted and allowed her to recover, but not this time. None of us knew that, including the paramedics who worked feverishly to save her life. I have carried tremendous guilt around for many years, always questioning my delay in calling 911 and placing her in a car to "get her home." Unfortunately, this information never helped me, the guilt as strong today as ever, but it does explain what was actually happening to Suzanne and for that I am grateful. As time went by, I slowly realized that my heart didn't break like it does when you break up with someone, actually it didn't break at all—it shattered. It broke into a thousand pieces, like a puzzle and putting it back together would be impossible. Each time I connected a piece the pain subsided a little, but there were so many pieces and it was so painful to connect them.

I cried every night for three hundred sixty-four days, every night I cried myself to sleep, even the nights I was too drunk to have conscious thoughts, the last thing to hit my pillow after my head was a teardrop. I stopped crying after three hundred sixty-four days, not because I wasn't as sad or miss her just as much as I did the day before. I stopped because it was time, I guess I had put enough pieces of the puzzle together and I was not going to cry on the anniversary of her death. The real obstacle to recovering was remembering and yet early on I promised to never forget her, but that was exactly the problem. It was precisely what was preventing me from starting over. There had to be a way to remember and not forget Suzanne and still move on with the rest of my life. And so, on the first anniversary of Suzanne's passing, I made a conscious decision. I decided to take her with me.

PART FOUR

It's Over

THE VERY FIRST THING YOU realize after you have lost someone you love is not how much you miss them or even how much you loved them or even how guilty you feel for not being a better husband, partner, friend or any other thing you can feel guilty about. The very first thing you think is that they are gone forever…no more holding her, kissing her, talking to her, or being with her ever again— ever. The finality is what makes it different from every other emotion we experience in life. My situation was no different than others. A loved one was here one minute and gone the next. I know all about heaven and I hope and pray that I will see her again, but my decision to take her with me while I was still here was imperative. She had to come with me. I never got the chance to say goodbye. Talking to her started almost immediately even though I didn't consciously admit taking her with me until the first anniversary of her passing.

Suzanne had told me on numerous occasions that if she passed away before me (which would never happen), I would be flirting at her funeral. "Holy shit, I would never do that. How the hell can you even think that?" Trust me, I never would, but I did think about it because she had put the thought in my head. I actually smiled internally as I caught the eye of an attractive woman in the crowd, and I bet Suzanne smiled too. Actually she laughed. It was an "I told you so" moment. After everything was over, I returned to our house and soon began sending out thank you notes for all the wonderful flowers and gifts and notes that we received, all supporting how wonderful Suzanne was in life.

For some strange reason, one I really can't explain to this day, I wanted a painting of Suzanne. Not just a painting, but one that looked like an Andy Warhol painting. How fucking crazy is that? But I soon found a picture of Suzanne and started researching places that might create what I was looking for. Many thought I was a little crazy, but one creative guy who could do unbelievable things on a computer soon put in front of me exactly what I was seeing in my mind. Not only that, but if you backed away from it, say 10 to 15 feet, it turned back into a picture…something about the human eye and its ability to focus.

Anyway, it was exactly what I wanted, and to this day hangs at the bottom of my steps where I say good morning and good night, which I have done every day and night for almost five years. I can look up from my desk where I have written the majority of this book and see her…sometimes a little uncomfortable but most times, comforting. Again, this was part of me taking her with me and it works.

Abstract style portrait of Suzanne

Suzanne was cremated and laid to rest at the National Cemetery of the Alleghenies and I will join her when my time comes. It is one of the most beautiful resting places in the world for veterans and their spouses. It covers 292 acres of rolling Western Pennsylvania hills and currently interns over 14,000 veterans and their spouses. I am told eventually more than 250,000 souls will find this as their final resting place. If you are ever driving in this part of the country (just off I-79, south of Pittsburgh) and you don't stop, you are missing a true American treasure.

National Cemetery of the Alleghenies

This treasure just happens to be located within minutes of that house that we purchased which affords me the opportunity to visit her, which I do often, but not often enough. Eventually, everything seemed to settle down as I continued working in Industrial Sales, and spending quality time with all of our children and doing the best I could with the nine grandchildren that now shared my life. Her children and mine became an integral part of my recovery and life after Suzanne. My two daughters have played a central role in that recovery and I am not capable of putting in words what they have meant to me. Suffice to say, they are the beautiful young ladies I so desperately needed to hold my hand and they have never failed to be there when I needed them.

In addition to providing support, I can also tell you that they were my wing woman when I needed "a date." Being out with a beautiful thirtysomething is like walking a puppy on the beach. I would never admit that I used them in this way, but I did, and they often laughed at how well it worked. So everything was fairly normal with the exception of my continuous struggle with prostate cancer.

I mentioned earlier in this story that one of the symptoms of Hormone replacement therapy was the growth of breast tissue, and I was no exception to this side effect. Allow me to state for the record that there is not a man alive that loves breasts more than I do. I just don't like them on me. It got to the point where I discussed my condition with my doctor. You might remember me mentioning radiation treatment earlier in this story and the fact that I asked for it. We felt, or he felt, that we might be able to shrink the tissue by using radiation, so I soon began treatments.

I also soon began to breakout in an unbelievable rash on my chest which I suspected was radiation poisoning, although no one actually admitted it. Take the worst itch and burn you have ever experienced and multiply it by one hundred and maybe you could equal this feeling. I cannot possibly convey how uncomfortable this became and how bad it looked. Scratching it only made it worse, but I couldn't help it. It was scratch or die. Eventually they prescribed a number of medications (creams) and special soaps and after months (yea...months) it began to clear up. So much for correcting my growing breast tissue problem which my doctors described as discomfort. I will leave it to your imagination to guess what I called it.

Anyway, I moved on accepting the fact that the treatment didn't work, and that I would just have to deal with the fact that I was growing boobs. As time went by, I eventually found the courage to ignore all the side effects and try to begin dating again. I eventually reverted back to my "Hi, I'm Denny" and for reasons not clear to me, I would add, "My wife passed away." If you would ever want to see a woman go from slightly interested to "Get the fuck away from me," use that as an opening line. I soon learned to eliminate the passing away part, and basically waited until questioned about my marital status. Even then, I was uncomfortable saying it, always feeling like I was looking for sympathy, which I was. I actually felt like I was sixteen-years-old, totally unsure, clumsy, and insecure. I hated how I felt and most, if not all of the women instinctively reacted with what I am sure was, "What an asshole."

One evening, I entered a local restaurant grabbing a seat next to two attractive ladies at the bar who soon initiated a conversation. I was actually there to meet a friend (more on her later) but was anxious to reciprocate and excited by their confident approach. Within minutes, I broke out in a sweat, the kind of sweat you get from mowing a lawn in August. Water was just falling off my face. I kept wiping it away hoping they did not notice, sure that they did, eventually cooling down to repeat, "Nice to meet you too," just as they made their escape. I guess I could have told them that I had prostate cancer and that hot flashes were one of the side effects, but if you think "Get the fuck away from me" was bad, can you imagine the response to dropping that nugget?

Understand that I am extremely immature and a residual effect of that is I honestly believe I am younger than I actually am—as in if age is a state of mind, I am fifty-three years old, maybe. That translates into women I am attracted to are too young, and they are not attracted to me and women who are attracted to me are too old and I am not attracted to them. How's that for superficial and completely out of touch, which probably explains the lack of touching which has become a significant part of my life.

Realizing this, I decided to grow up, admit my age and the fact that I had cancer and be slightly more understanding, and let someone else handle it. And so, that's exactly what I did being convinced by my youngest daughter to sign up for a dating service. Holy shit, I can't believe I did that. Actually, I didn't. She did. I just picked out the pictures of the ladies I liked, and she actually ran the format, often helping me with the appropriate thing to say—as she typed away on the computer.

My new attitude in conjunction with my daughter running a dating service for me, produced moderate success. A date here, a short relationship there, but nothing that made the relationship needle jump. Along the way, my friend, who just happened to be beautiful, satisfied my desire to spend at least an occasional evening, laughing, talking, listening, and sharing life experiences. We had so much fun together it was difficult for me to separate the friendship from the attraction. Luckily, it was not difficult for her as she always maintained "we are only friends" which means exactly what you are thinking it means. Like a dumb ass, I continued to flirt with her between "friendly discussions" eventually being turned down so many times that I looked at her and said, "Look, I have a system or standard where if I hit on someone three times and get turned down three times, then I just give up. So you win. We will just be friends." She looked at me and laughed. "Well, that's great except this is the sixth time you have hit on me, so maybe you might want to consider recalculating your standard."

That was it. I had not only violated my own self-imposed standard, I had infringed on our friendship, believing my feelings for her would overcome her feelings (or lack of) for me. We soon set the record straight, more difficult for me than her, but critical in saving a relationship. She had taught me the difference between loving someone, and being in love with someone and I was grateful to settle for "just friends." I needed a friend, and so did she and we remain the closest of friends to this day, me still trying to teach myself to ignore beautiful when it is staring me right in the face.

Around this time, my prostate cancer took a turn for the worse. One day while on a family vacation, I complained about my situation (which I rarely did) when a family member offered up that "Nobody dies from prostate cancer anymore." I held my tongue knowing that more than thirty-two thousand men had died from it just that year. I was actually curious how such a statement could be made until my research made me aware of the fact that since the advent of PSA tests, prostate cancer deaths have been cut by a third. That, however, makes the conclusions by the United States Preventative Services Task Force in 2011 of limiting PSA tests, even more controversial.

Allow me to give you some additional statistics. There are 220,800 new cases of prostate cancers diagnosed every year in the United States. The American Cancer Society estimates that one in seven American men will be diagnosed with prostate cancer in their lifetime. One in thirty-six men will die from prostate cancer accounting for 22 percent of all male deaths from cancer. Prostate cancer is the most common cancer in American men. Obviously, I am not a doctor nor am I any type of clinician that can argue for or against any medical test. But I am alive, and my advice is get a PSA test! Years ago, as I began researching information for this book, I came upon an article written by David Kushma, who at the time was the editor of The Blade of Toledo, the sister newspaper to the *Pittsburgh Post-Gazette*. I tried but failed to capture his feelings concerning the conclusions of the task force, so I ultimately decided to borrow his. Writing an article in October 2011, or at least a reprinted version at that time, he concluded the following: "Amid the mass of scientific evidence the task force has assembled against the PSA test, I can offer just one statistically insignificant yet stubborn fact in its (PSA test) favor. I'm *here* to talk about it." My thoughts exactly. Several years after Suzanne's passing, my PSA began to climb, eventually reaching 396 (yea, that is not a misprint). It was at this time that I decided on a different treatment although this increase was caused for two distinctively different reasons. One was my cancer cells were becoming increasingly more resistant to my treatment and, two, I had begun limiting my recommended dosages. I know that sounds really stupid, which it was, but I was tired of feeling like shit and needed a break from the side effects.

So once again, it was time for a bone scan and a CAT scan to ensure that my cancer had not metastasized to anything given the fact that I had a PSA of 396, when I didn't even have a prostate, was more than a little worrisome. After all the tests cleared me again, I visited with my doctor who gave me a couple of options. We eventually settled on a relatively new drug which would be used in conjunction with my quarterly hormone replacement shots. I was to swallow four pills in succession (160 mgs) at basically the same time daily. I used the word swallow for a reason as these pills were huge, and I had problems taking an aspirin. As you might guess, the side effects from all of this increased but it beat the alternative.

Within a couple of months, my PSA went from 396 to 94.49. I wish you could have been there for that party!

Those numbers progressed over the next several months to 28 and then 14 and then 2.4 which was my last reading as I write this. That represents my lowest reading in eight years and basically lowers the chances of my cancer metastasizing. The hot flashes have increased to the point that I can hear Suzanne laughing especially after some specific situations. Recently I was meeting with a banker discussing some form of CD investment when sweat began rolling off my face. It got worse as I spotted the cameras, thinking if someone was monitoring them, they would surely arrest me on the spot. She never mentioned anything, but I am sure the banker reviewed the tapes to ensure the details were correct soon after I left. By the time I got to my car, I was laughing out loud, and so was Suzanne, which made me laugh even harder. In addition to the hot flashes, the incontinence, which I had worked to control over the years, suddenly became a real problem. If I looked at water, I had to piss. The only exception being if I was sitting down. If I was standing or laughing or coughing, I wanted a bathroom near. Actually this problem is part of the consequences from having your prostate removed as it serves as kind of a plug for men. I learned early on to work on muscle control. It was that or quit drinking beer and that was unacceptable, so I was fanatical about learning to control my bladder.

Early on Suzanne and I would be watching a show like *The Bachelor* (her pick, not mine) and the first thing out of my mouth when the date ended up in some remote location was, "Where do they go to the bathroom?" She would roll on the floor, often anticipating me saying it. I never disappointed. Unfortunately, another side effect that increased (are we having fun yet?) was the growth of breast tissue. It finally got to the point where I had to limit my clothing choices as some shirts enhanced the problem while others limited my self-consciousness. It finally got to the point where I got mad and decided I needed to take control of the situation. This shit was controlling almost everything I did, and I finally had enough. It was time to fight back. In addition to the vanity part of this, there was some concern about breast cancer which if you haven't heard, can occur in men.

So I finally got up enough courage to visit a surgeon, convinced that I would be the only man in the waiting room, full of women either getting enhanced or correcting some kind of problem, all with eyes on me wondering what the fuck is up with this guy. Believe me, I saw that waiting room in my dreams like some episode of *Sex and the City*. Many nights prior to my visit, I would wake up not really knowing if it was a hot flash or a panic attack, soon realizing it was probably both. Like most apprehension however, none of that came to fruition as I entered the office occupied by women, men, and young adults. Nothing unusual. I was just another patient. The exam however, proved that some of the apprehension was actually justified. My surgeon entered the examining room accompanied by an attractive surgeon in training. She was very nice and didn't say much but I still felt a little uncomfortable as my surgeon began pushing and prodding my man boobs, explaining the details of what he hoped to accomplish.

As I sat there experiencing this, I suddenly thought about my own trips to second base and almost instantly reached for my shirt wanting to "cover up," simultaneously thankful that my past conquests did not elicit a similar response. As I entered the parking garage and got in my car, I suddenly realized that I had just committed to having a radical mastectomy, that thought being followed by Suzanne's, "You are out of your mind." How can you top a moment like that? My daughter (a nurse) accompanied me to the hospital and was by my side before being taken to the operating room. Nothing, not one story, could ever compete with the many hysterical situations she has experienced over her many years of nursing. But when the processing nurse asked me what I was there for during their FBI interrogation, I answered after some confusion and deliberation, "I guess I am having a boob job." It was all my daughter could do to keep a straight face.

I knew my condition was called gynecomastia but for the most part, I try not to espouse words I cannot spell or correctly pronounce. As I was being wheeled down the hall to the operation room, I almost told them to stop. I almost told them to turn around. I had been through my share of surgeries and I thought, "What the hell am I doing? I don't have to do this. This is not saving my life." Thank god it was not a long trip as I soon realized that this was important "to me." Maybe it wasn't important or perceived to be important by others, but it was really important to me. It was one of the few things that my cancer had caused that

I could fix. I needed to send a message to my cancer cells, "Take a suck of that."

The surgery went well. My man boobs were gone, and although the scars and what was left of my chest looks pretty bad, I am being patient and anticipating decent results in the coming months. Once again, I have gained a continued empathy for women. Shit, it is amazing how much I have learned over these years and how differently I now perceive the opposite sex. I have always had a healthy respect for women starting with the incredible example set by my mother. But I never anticipated learning this much or experiencing this much. How in the hell could you ever imagine this? Somehow, I think my guardian angels wanted to teach me a lesson, not as a punishment, but as a stimulus to be a more understanding father and grandfather to my daughters and granddaughters. Imagine that! So I continued to be monitored for my cancer, realizing that I have been fighting this for over eight years. I will never beat it, the cells will never leave my body and will continue to grow, which is why I put up with all this shit and will as long as I am able. Certainly, I hope that someday, something will be discovered that will rid my body of these cancer cells but in the meantime, the longer I put off any chance of metastasizing, the better.

So, as I come to the end of this story, I would like to explain why I wrote it in the first place. As I previously mentioned, it all started as a story about prostate cancer as I sincerely wanted to reach as many people as possible (men and women) and I soon realized that maybe more people would be exposed if it was humorous and interesting versus simply explaining medical conditions. In addition to providing medical information in a slightly humorous way, I also wanted very much to include Suzanne's story, as her condition, although maybe a little rare, might possibly be more prevalent than I suspected. I hope in some way that enough people will now become aware of this unique heart condition and possibly follow up with an exam, especially if there is any history in their family. In the end Suzanne did not make it, but very talented doctors gave her three years, instead of three weeks. While writing this story, I thought about other people who have experienced tragic losses and how we all deal with those losses differently. Some people shy away from memories, staying away from anything that reminds them of a lost love. I crossed that bridge convinced initially that anything that reminded me of Suzanne would be too painful to deal with, even preparing to sell our house. I could not possibly mow the lawn where I laid trying to breathe life back into her body. How the hell could I do that? I could not sleep in the same bedroom or enjoy time on the back patio or deck where we had so many great times, the best being the night she said, "I love this house."

At some point, however, I realized that the opposite was true. I needed to keep everything about her in my life. I could not survive without it, without her. I just knew how lucky I was to have had her in my life, and I sure as hell was not going to give her up because she died. I was still here, and by God, she was going with me, like it or not. I also knew that I am a better person than I otherwise would have been without her in my life. After all, her last words were "Take me home," so if I leave our home, in a way I am leaving her, and that thought hurts more than staying. So, as I sit here staring at the portrait of Suzanne that has shadowed and inspired me through this whole process, I take another deep breath, deeper than the many I have taken to complete this story. At this point, my thoughts are amazingly concise and clear. I hope she is proud of me. I can't begin to describe how proud I am of her. I don't know how you say goodbye so quickly. Maybe that's why I never got the chance. I do know, however, that she knew it was me, as I knew it was her, and we knew it was about us, when suddenly we also knew it was over.

April 8, 2018,
Promise Kept.

EPILOGUE

HAVING NEVER CONSIDERED AN EPILOGUE, in the end I found myself thinking about a conclusion or a summary. Especially now that a significant amount of time has passed since I completed my story. That is due in part by procrastination and in part because of extensive research concerning the editing and publishing of my story. In addition, some things have changed with my prostate cancer, some new treatments have been discovered for prostate cancer and I have begun a new relationship with a wonderful woman. All of these things have caused delay.

Allow me first to discuss my new relationship. Just after the fifth anniversary of my wife's passing, I had pretty much resigned myself to the fact that I probably had loved for the last time. I had accepted the fact that my life would be fulfilled by children, grandchildren, family and friends—and that was more than okay. Coming to the realization however, left me feeling a little defeated. Was I really giving up on love or was I trying to convince myself that it didn't matter? Secretly I still wanted to share my life with a woman that I loved, and then just as that thought was fading, the most wonderful woman in the world entered my life. All of a sudden, I had met a lady that shared many of my interests and a woman who continues to suggest healthy improvements to my life. A woman who has listened and genuinely cared about my condition. A woman who has responded with compassion and understanding, far beyond anything I could ever imagine.

The honesty between us and the level of mature conversations defy the time we have spent together. In a very short period of time, we have discussed more sensitive subjects than most couples discuss in a lifetime, trust me, I am an expert. One day, I hope to publish all that we discovered and experienced, but for now it is all too private and sensitive. It is imperative that I protect her although the tears and laughter associated with a recent trip have certainly peaked my interest in writing and educating again. We will see. In the interim, we will find comfort in a mutual love and respect.

As I mentioned, I also wanted to include an update on my prostate cancer status. Once again, my PSA levels have increased, this time reaching 29. And once again, a new drug is available. I may begin treatment in early 2019. The increase in PSA seems to have occurred because once again the cancer cells, (I now call them Pac-Men), have become more resistant to my current treatment. Although my current drug and the new drug, (I anticipate taking both), work to prevent my cancer cells from growing, I have come to understand that the more they increase the harder they become to control.

In other words, a lower PSA is easier to control than a higher PSA. The good news is we have lowered my PSA from a very high level in the past, so hopefully we can accomplish that again. Keep in mind, the whole reason for controlling the growth is to prevent metastasis, (particularly bone cancer), in patients with non-metastatic castration-resistant prostate cancer or MN-CRPC, which is what I have. Delay is what I have been doing for nine years. At this point, delay is the most important word in the English language, as the development of bone metastasis certainly makes my prognosis worse. Delay doesn't sound like a great option, but for now it's all I or anyone else with this condition has. I've come to have a deep respect for delays, trust me they are not all bad.

In addition to new medications being developed to treat prostate cancer, there have also been breakthroughs in treatments, treatments that did not exist or were not employed nine years ago. One such treatment is called proton therapy. Proton therapy has actually been used for years in the treatment of brain, spine, and eye cancers. Proton beam therapy is similar to conventional radiation, or x-rays, but it allows doctors to be more precise in directing treatment. Consider an x-ray or radiation like a shot gun and proton beam as a single shot, more controlled and more precise with less damage to surrounding tissue. Having never experienced this treatment, I can only refer readers to published reports, as I have no opinion one way or another. The best report is put out by the University of California at Berkeley school of public health. You can simply google "Proton therapy for prostate cancer" and find the heading that reads, "Does Proton Beam Therapy for Prostate Cancer Live Up to its Promise"; Health UC Berkeley. The obvious warning is always consult your physician as even new treatments carry risks and side effects. My only advice is get as much information as you possibly can, and get multiple opinions.

So as I conclude this summary, I need to emphasize that I never once believed that this idle threat or promise would actually be completed. At the same time, determination overcame my casual attitude, and in the end the project took on a unique significance. It not only served as an emotional release that I so desperately needed, but more importantly, I might have succeeded far beyond my original intent and helped one person. Imagine that.

ABOUT THE AUTHOR

D.J. CONNORS GREW UP IN Pittsburgh, Pennsylvania. He is a graduate of Xavier University in Cincinnati, Ohio and served in the U.S. Air Force, stationed in Thailand during the Vietnam War. He is a proud father to three and grandfather to eleven.